Mrs. Frk

It Happened at
PICKLE LAKE

by Christel Kleitsch
and True Kelley

DUTTON CHILDREN'S BOOKS

NEW YORK

For Maisie, my climbing girl

C.K.

To Barbara and Alfred Wheeler at Salmon Lake

T.K.

Speedsters is a trademark of Dutton Children's Books.

Text copyright © 1993 by Christel Kleitsch
Illustrations copyright © 1993 by True Kelley

Library of Congress Cataloging-in-Publication Data

Kleitsch, Christel.
  It happened at Pickle Lake / by Christel Kleitsch and [illustrated
by] True Kelley.—1st ed.
      p.   cm.
  Summary: Rachel would rather be vacationing in Florida with a
friend than camping with Mom and Dad, until she climbs a mountain.
  ISBN 0-525-45058-0
  [1. Camping—Fiction. 2. Vacations—Fiction. 3. Family life—
Fiction.] I. Kelley, True, ill. II. Title.
PZ7.K67837It 1993   92-44231
[Fic]—dc20   CIP
                                                              AC

Published in the United States by Dutton Children's Books,
a division of Penguin Books USA Inc.
375 Hudson Street, New York, New York 10014

Printed in U.S.A.   First Edition
10 9 8 7 6 5 4 3 2 1

Chapter One

"Florida!" I yelled into the phone.

You mean Disneyworld? Beaches? Flamingos? THAT Florida?

My friend Maggie laughed. "Yes, *that* Florida," she said. "Do you want to come?"

"Yes! Yes! Yes!" I said. "I'll tell my parents and call you right back."

I ran to the kitchen. Mom and Dad were looking at a map. I told them about Maggie's invitation.

Ahhh... Here it is : Pickle Lake.

GUESS WHAT? Maggie's family has invited me to Florida! In two weeks!

Mom and Dad looked at each other.
Mom made a face.

"Guess what?" Dad said. "We want to take you to a cabin on Pickle Lake—in two weeks."

I had to think fast.

"I know," I said. "You guys go to Pickle Lake, and I'll go to Florida."

That way, we'll all be happy!

They both shook their heads.

And that was that. Nothing I could say would change their minds. All Dad talked about for the next two weeks was how much fun we would have.

I knew Mom would spend the whole vacation with her nose in a book.

"Then it's just you and me, Rachel," Dad said, giving me a big hug.

I tried to sound happy. But it's hard when you're being squeezed half to death.

It was pouring rain on the day we left.

We had to drive about a million miles to get to Pickle Lake.

Directions to Pickle Lake:
Go south on Highway 89
North for 8 miles, then
turn right onto Dill Drive.
Make sharp left at third
fork, then go right
at Ketchup Creek.
Go 2 miles to first left,
Relish Road; continue
past Sour Street to
Pickle Lake Road. Go
another 400 feet
and you're there.

N ←→ S Rt. 89 North

Dill Drive

Relish Rd.
Ketchup Creek
Pickle Lake Rd.
Sour Street

Rusted was more like it. The place was a dump!

And it was no better inside.

This was what I gave up Florida for?

Chapter Two

A strange noise woke me up in the
middle of the night. I grabbed for Homer,
my octopus.

"Don't worry, Homer," I whispered. "It's
only—"

"I heard a scary sound," I said.

Dad was still sleeping. Of course. Mom poked him.

Dad rolled over and put his pillow over his head. Mom poked him again. He rolled over again.

And then he
fell out of bed.

That woke him up.

We went outside to look around. It had stopped raining. It was really dark.

"That's the sound!" I said. "What is that?"
Dad said it was a bird.

"It sounds lovely and sad," said Mom.

"Listen, Rachel, what else do you hear?"

There were chirping noises all around.

"See, that's what living in the city does to a kid," Dad said to Mom.

"Fooled you," I said. "I know it's crickets."

"Look up!" said Mom. "Isn't it
wonderful?"

I had never seen so many stars in my
life. Millions of them twinkling in the deep,
black sky.

Dad pointed across the lake at a big dark hill. "That's Silver Peak," he said. "It's the highest spot around here."

We're going to climb it, Rachel. You and I.

Are you kidding?

Me? Climb all the way up there?

Suddenly I was surrounded by . . .

MOSQUITOES!

I slapped at my cheek.

And my arm. And my neck.

And my leg.

I snuggled under my blankets with
Homer. I was almost asleep when I heard
something else.

This was one nature sound I knew.

Chapter Three

The next morning the sun was shining.
The air was warm. Things were looking up.

"Shall we climb Silver Peak or canoe to
the end of the lake?" Dad said.

I looked out the window at Silver Peak.
"Let's go canoeing," I said quickly.

Dad sat in the back of the canoe—he called it the stern.

It was tricky climbing in. The canoe was very tippy.

Dad paddled us into a little bay. At the end it turned into a marsh.

It was so neat. There was so much to see.

Kingfisher

great blue heron

dragonfly

cattails

water snake

painted turtle

minnows

water boatman bug

Dad showed
me how to hold the
paddle, how to pull it
through the water, and
how to lift it out.

The paddle felt
big and clumsy.

WHOOPS!

Come here,
paddle...

Dad flipped the canoe over and helped
me climb in.

I was a mess.
I felt really stupid, too.

Dad held the paddle out to me.

I shook my head. "Canoeing is too hard."

Dad laughed. "Come on, honey. You'll get the hang of it."

I didn't like it when he laughed at me. "I don't want to," I said.

And that was the end of my canoe lesson.

Chapter Four

The next morning Dad announced that he and I were climbing Silver Peak. He didn't even ask me if I wanted to.

Dad packed our lunch. He kept adding more and more food.

I looked at Silver Peak through the
window. It was so high. It would take
rocket fuel to get me to the top.

We canoed across the lake to the Silver Peak trail. Dad didn't bug me once about paddling.

"The first two hours of the climb are supposed to be easy," he said. "But the last hour to the top is pretty steep."

The trail was
a little path through
the woods. I wondered if
there were any bears around.
But bears were not the problem.

It was bugs—millions of them.
Mosquitoes, blackflies, deerflies.

We stopped and put on some bug
repellent.

"You smell like a dead rat!" I said to Dad.

He made a face. "So do you!"

We both laughed.

We walked for a long, long time.
But when I looked at my watch,
it was only an hour later.
I couldn't believe it.

My twenty-three bug bites were itching me like crazy.

We had to climb over big rocks. I accidentally grabbed onto a thorny branch.

The sharp thorns really hurt.

We came to a tiny stream. There was a mossy log lying across it. As I stepped onto the log, it rolled.

Dad leaned over me. "Are you all right, Rachel?"

I had tears in my eyes.

Chapter Five

"I want to go back down."

"But, Rachel," Dad said, "we're almost to the top."

"I don't care," I said. "I'm tired."

"I know you can make it," said Dad.

"Well, *I* know I can't," I said. "I'm going down."

Dad lost his temper. "That does it!" he yelled. "Yesterday canoeing was too hard for you. Today you want to quit in the middle of this climb."

YOU'RE JUST SPOILED!

I AM NOT!

"You just want to go to Florida and lie around on some beach," Dad said.

Boy, was I mad! I covered my ears with my hands.

Dad shouted louder. So I stuck out my tongue at him.

He turned and stomped off down the trail. "I'll meet you at the bottom," he called back to me.

I was so angry, I started to cry.

Dad's footsteps stopped. I knew he was waiting for me a little way down the trail. Waiting for me to come running after him—like a baby.

Well, he would be waiting for a long time.

I looked at the trail. I would show Dad that he was wrong about me.

I CAN CLIMB THIS DUMB MOUNTAIN!

I started walking up the hill. I hardly felt tired at all.

Near the top it got all rocky. There were no trees, just some blueberry bushes.

I scrambled up on my hands and knees. I scraped my knuckles, but I made it.

Finally I was standing on the very top
of Silver Peak. I could see forever in all
directions.

The wind whistled softly in my ears. It felt cool on my bug bites. And you know what? Pickle Lake *was* shaped like a pickle!

49

After a while Dad came up behind me.
He put his arm around me.

We sat quietly on a big rock for a long
time, just looking and looking.

Then I heard snuffling sounds. "Look,
Dad!" I whispered.

"Shhh," Dad said very softly.

I didn't move. I didn't even breathe. I could hardly believe it. A real, live wild bear. It was nothing like seeing a bear in a zoo.

Then the bear looked up. Right at us.
I was scared. I squeezed Dad's hand
hard.

The bear snorted. It kept staring at us.

Then it turned and walked quickly down
into the woods.

Dad and I both let out a long breath.

"Wasn't that great?" Dad said.

I nodded. "Magical!"

Thanks for bringing me up here, Dad.

You're welcome, but I didn't bring you. You brought yourself.

"Let's leave a sign to show that we were here," Dad said.

I found a stone that sparkled like diamonds in the sun. Dad found a white feather. We put them on the rock where we had been sitting.

Then we ate our lunch. All of it.

Chapter Six

That night after supper we made a fire near the lake. Mom got out a bag of marshmallows.

"You deserve a treat after your big climb today," said Mom.

"She sure does," said Dad. "She was great."

Thank you,
fans.
Thank you.
Thank you.

Mom and Dad clapped. I was fooling around, but I *was* proud that I had made it to the top of Silver Peak.

I ate thirteen toasted marshmallows.

An all-time record!

"What are your plans for tomorrow?"
Mom asked.

"Why don't we climb Silver Peak again—
all of us?" I said.

But Dad was tired.

Are you kidding? My legs are killing me!

Maybe we'd see that bear again!

Mom winked at me. "I've got a good book you can borrow," she told Dad.

"How about more canoeing?" I said. After climbing Silver Peak, I knew I could do anything.

"Hey, look at that!" Mom said.

Right over Silver Peak was the biggest, yellowest moon I had ever seen.

Dad started singing a
funny song. Mom joined in.

Won't you come and
do a moon dance with me?
We'll boogie down
the Milky Way ...

Moose dance?

Loon dance?

Dad held out his hand to me.

So Dad and I danced on the shore.

My dad is so crazy sometimes. But that's
one of the things I like about him.

"I call this the Pickle Lake polka," Dad said while we were dancing.

I giggled.

So what if I didn't get a summer vacation in Florida? I still had a *great* time.